Auntie Tigress

and Other Favorite Chinese Folktales

RETOLD BY
Gia-Zhen Wang

ILLUSTRATED BY
Eva Wang

TRANSLATED BY
ANNIE KUNG

Purple Bear Books
New York

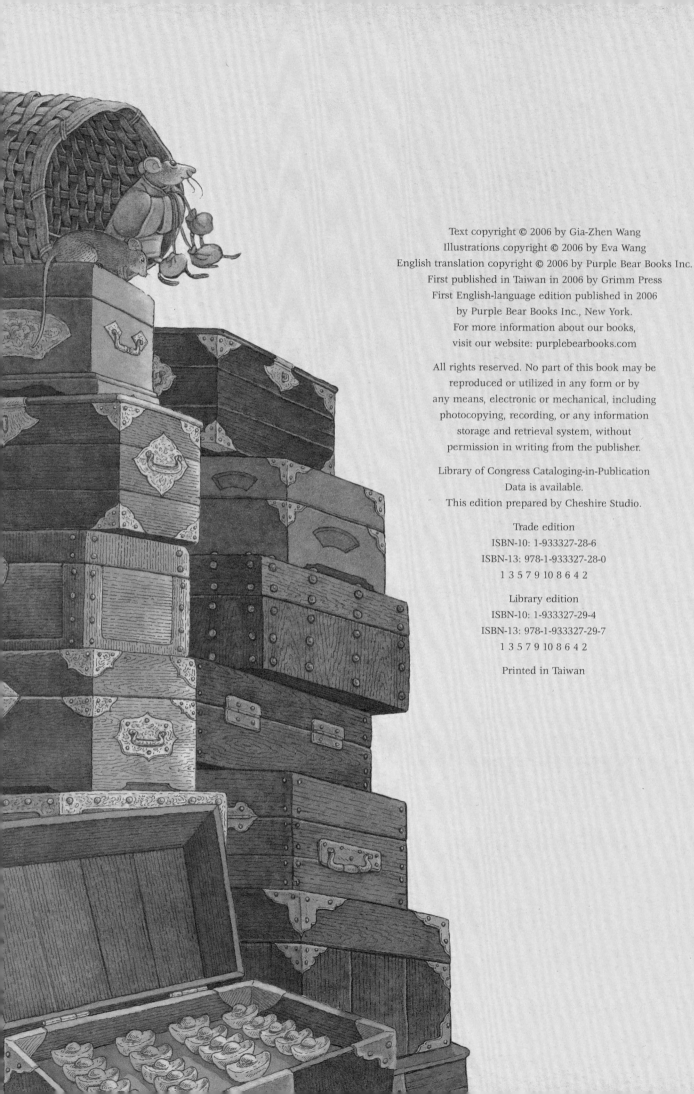

Library of Congress Cataloging-in-Publication
Data is available.
This edition prepared by Cheshire Studio.

Trade edition
ISBN-10: 1-933327-28-6
ISBN-13: 978-1-933327-28-0
1 3 5 7 9 10 8 6 4 2

Library edition
ISBN-10: 1-933327-29-4
ISBN-13: 978-1-933327-29-7
1 3 5 7 9 10 8 6 4 2

Printed in Taiwan

Contents

Auntie Tigress

High up in the mountains lived an old, old Tigress who had been on Earth for so long that she had mastered the art of transforming herself into an old lady.

The Tigress was sly and cunning. She had long sharp teeth, and when she was hungry, she would come down from the mountains to prey on people. She was especially fond of tender, juicy children.

After she had gobbled up a child, she would collect, as a trophy, the child's golden locket, pendant, bracelet, or earrings. The Tigress decorated her immense cape with these souvenirs. She loved the clinging, clanging sounds they made as she stomped through the mountains. They seemed to say to the world, "Here comes the Tigress, the greatest child-eating monster of all!"

4

One day, the Tigress was hungry and headed down the mountains to find a plump little child for dinner. She came to a house at the foot of a hill and hid behind a tree.

A mother called to her daughter, "MeiMei, my sweet girl, I'm taking your father his dinner. He needs to finish harvesting the crops. Your great-aunt from over the mountain is coming to stay with you. I left some buns in the kitchen for you to share."

"I've never met Great-aunt," said MeiMei. "How will I know it's her?"

"She will call you by name," said her mother. "And she is bringing you a pair of pretty red shoes. Be good. Stay inside and lock the doors," she added, and hurried on her way.

The Tigress drooled at the sight of lovely MeiMei and the shiny golden locket she wore around her neck. She raced to the door, but MeiMei had already locked it, just as she'd been told.

"That MeiMei is a clever girl," grumbled the Tigress. "But I'll get her to open that door."

7

The Tigress hid in the bushes and waited until she heard MeiMei's great-aunt coming up the path. Then the Tigress leaped up and let out a ferocious roar! Poor Great-aunt was so frightened that she fainted.

The Tigress tied Great-aunt to a tree and quickly transformed herself into an old woman. She picked up the satchel with the pair of pretty red shoes in it and hurried back to MeiMei's house.

"Open the doors, my dear," she called in through the window.

"Who are you?" asked MeiMei.

"Why, I am your great-aunt," the Tigress replied.

MeiMei peered at her closely. "Mother said that Great-aunt would know my name and would bring me a gift."

"Oh, yes," said the Tigress, opening the satchel. "Look, MeiMei, I brought you a pair of pretty red shoes. Now be a good girl and let me in."

Relieved that this was indeed her great-aunt, MeiMei unlocked the doors.

MeiMei led Auntie Tigress into the kitchen and offered her some of the delicious buns. The Tigress was not interested in eating one. It was MeiMei that she wanted! Just to win her trust, the Tigress reached for a bun anyway. But when she saw a little mouse on the plate she fell to the floor, cowering in terror. Who could have imagined that of all the creatures on Earth, the mighty Tigress feared only mice.

MeiMei burst out laughing. "Oh, Great-aunt, how can you be afraid of a little mouse?"

Furious and embarrassed, the Tigress picked up a long bamboo stick and waved it at the mouse.

Speedy, nimble mouse! He jumped up and down and left and right and finally ducked into one of MeiMei's new red shoes.

"Now I've got you!" cried the Tigress as she raised the stick to strike him.

MeiMei wanted to save the poor little creature. "Stop! Don't ruin my new red shoes!" she said, distracting the Tigress long enough for the mouse to scamper out of the house.

The Tigress was furious about the mouse's escape and she stomped and screamed. When she did, MeiMei caught a glimpse of a tail peeking out from under the Tigress's long skirt.

Then Auntie Tigress went into the bedroom and called to MeiMei, "Come and take a nap with me."

Now that MeiMei knew Great-aunt was really a Tigress, she wasn't going near her! "First let me try on my new red shoes," she said, and she quickly put on the shoes and headed for the door. But the Tigress had blocked it with a boulder, and MeiMei could not open the door.

The Tigress again called for MeiMei to join her in the bedroom. MeiMei thought for a moment and replied, "I need to go to the outhouse first."

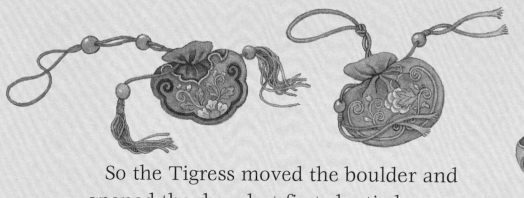

So the Tigress moved the boulder and opened the door, but first she tied a rope around MeiMei's waist to make sure the little girl could not run away.

Out in the yard, MeiMei tried to untie the heavy rope, but her hands were too small and delicate to loosen the knots. As she sat crying in frustration, a little mouse crawled out of a basket and started gnawing at the rope. It was the very mouse that MeiMei had rescued!

Soon MeiMei was free! The mouse thanked her for saving his life and gave her three little sachets. But before he could tell MeiMei what they were for, the Tigress came charging out of the house, sending MeiMei and the mouse scurrying away.

MeiMei ran into the bamboo forest. Her steps were much smaller than the Tigress's huge strides and, in no time at all, the Tigress was upon her. As she looked over her shoulder at the fierce creature, MeiMei tripped and dropped the red sachet.

A little red bean rolled out of the bag, bounced three times, and suddenly turned into hundreds of red beans that rolled all over the ground.

When the Tigress stepped on them, she slipped and fell with a loud *thud*. She landed so hard that a few of her teeth were jarred loose. As the Tigress roared in pain, MeiMei ran away, her footsteps taunting the Tigress.

The Tigress got up, gritted her loose teeth, and raced after MeiMei.

When she caught up to her, MeiMei was less afraid, for now she knew that the mouse's sachets were magical. She opened the blue sachet and threw it behind her. One slender sewing needle flew out of the bag,

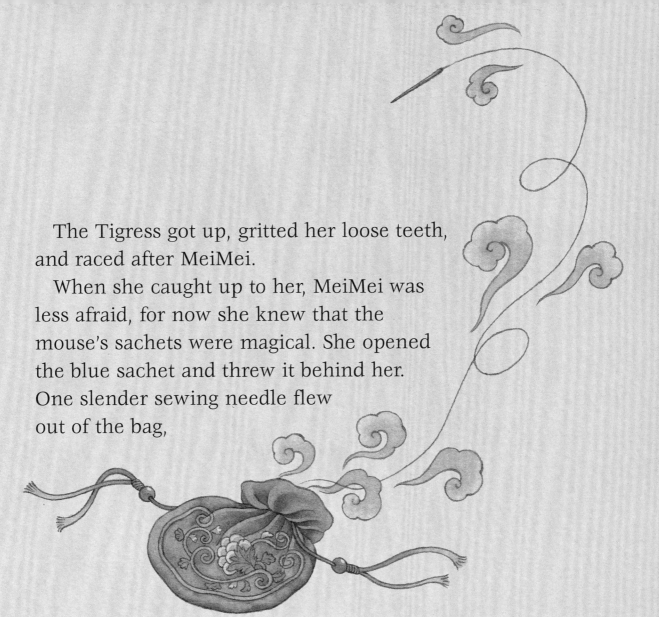

twirled in the air, and turned into hundreds of needles. The needles instantly burrowed into the ground and sprouted into plants that looked like soft peacock feathers—but were as sharp as needles.

As the Tigress ran through the feathery plants, they pricked her all over and she fell to the ground, writhing in pain.

MeiMei kept running, her footsteps taunting the Tigress once again.

As she pulled the sharp feathers out of her feet, the Tigress swore to catch MeiMei and gobble her up!

Once again the Tigress caught up to the little girl quickly, but, just as she reached out to grab her, MeiMei opened the golden sachet and tossed it over her shoulder.

A fine golden hair wafted out and turned into hundreds of mice with golden fur. The mice swarmed over the Tigress, quickly covering her from head to toe. Roaring in fear, the Tigress turned and raced back to the mountains.

Indeed, she was so terrified of the mice that she did not show her face for five hundred years!

MeiMei ran out of the bamboo forest and met her mother, who was hurrying home along the path. They untied Great-aunt and helped her back to the house. Before long, MeiMei's father finished the harvest and returned home, too, and they all lived happily ever after.

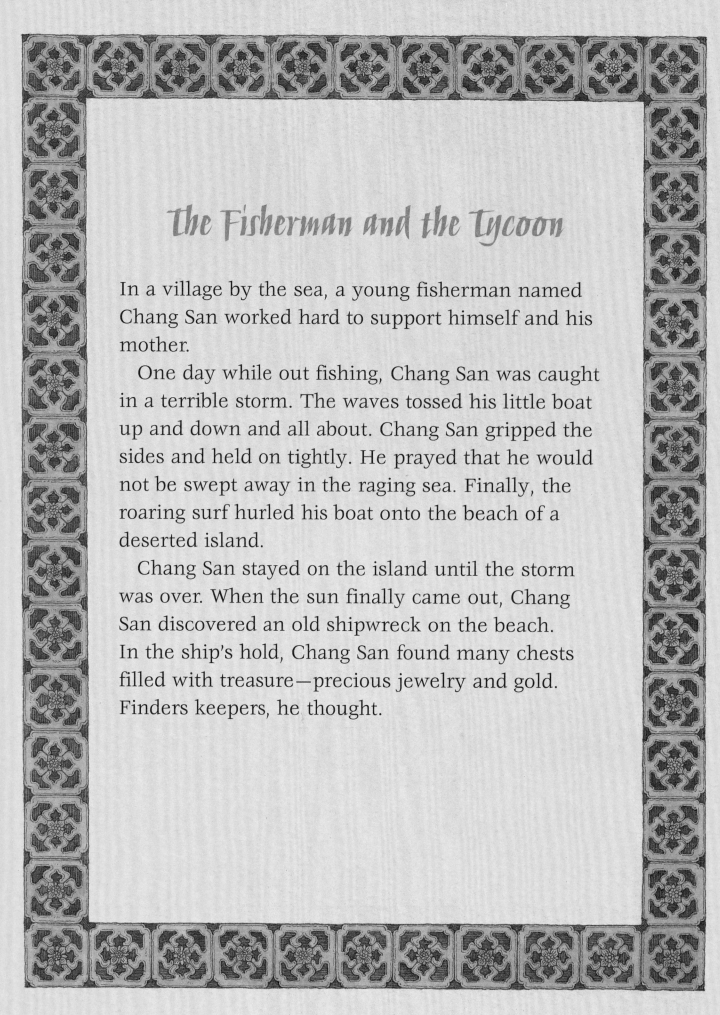

The Fisherman and the Tycoon

In a village by the sea, a young fisherman named Chang San worked hard to support himself and his mother.

One day while out fishing, Chang San was caught in a terrible storm. The waves tossed his little boat up and down and all about. Chang San gripped the sides and held on tightly. He prayed that he would not be swept away in the raging sea. Finally, the roaring surf hurled his boat onto the beach of a deserted island.

Chang San stayed on the island until the storm was over. When the sun finally came out, Chang San discovered an old shipwreck on the beach. In the ship's hold, Chang San found many chests filled with treasure—precious jewelry and gold. Finders keepers, he thought.

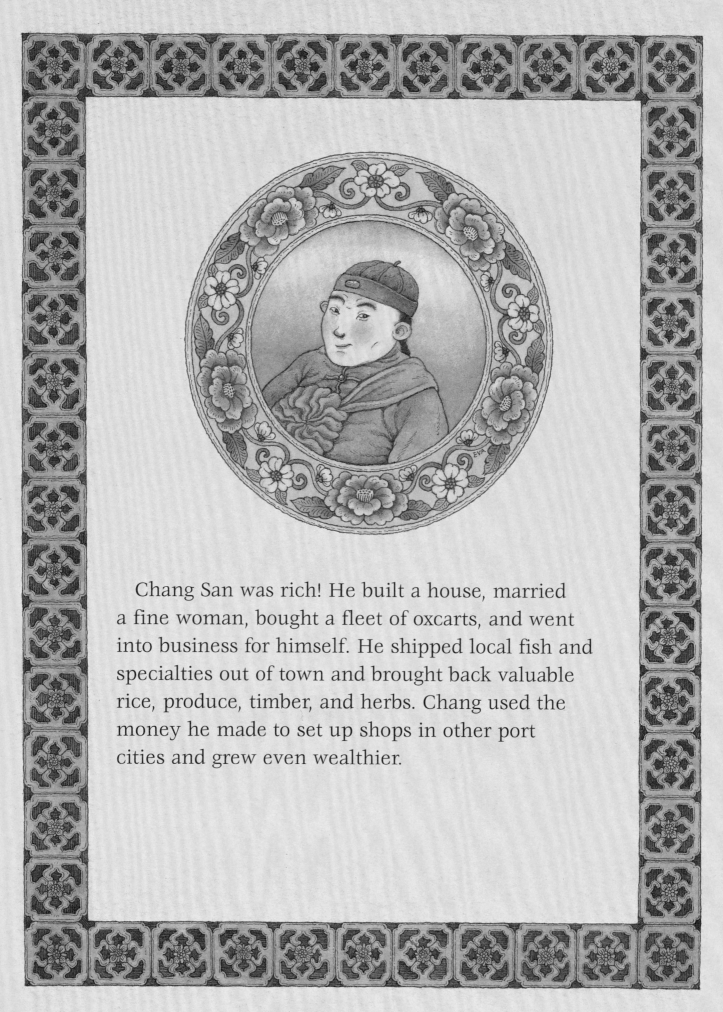

Chang San was rich! He built a house, married
a fine woman, bought a fleet of oxcarts, and went
into business for himself. He shipped local fish and
specialties out of town and brought back valuable
rice, produce, timber, and herbs. Chang used the
money he made to set up shops in other port
cities and grew even wealthier.

Most of the land in the village was owned by a man named Lu who had always been the richest tycoon in town until Chang San became wealthy. This filled Lu with a jealous rage. Whenever he heard the villagers gossiping about Chang's wealth—wondering whether Chang or Lu was richer—Lu would rant and storm in fury. "Chang San! A lowly fisherman! A nobody! How could anyone compare him to me?"

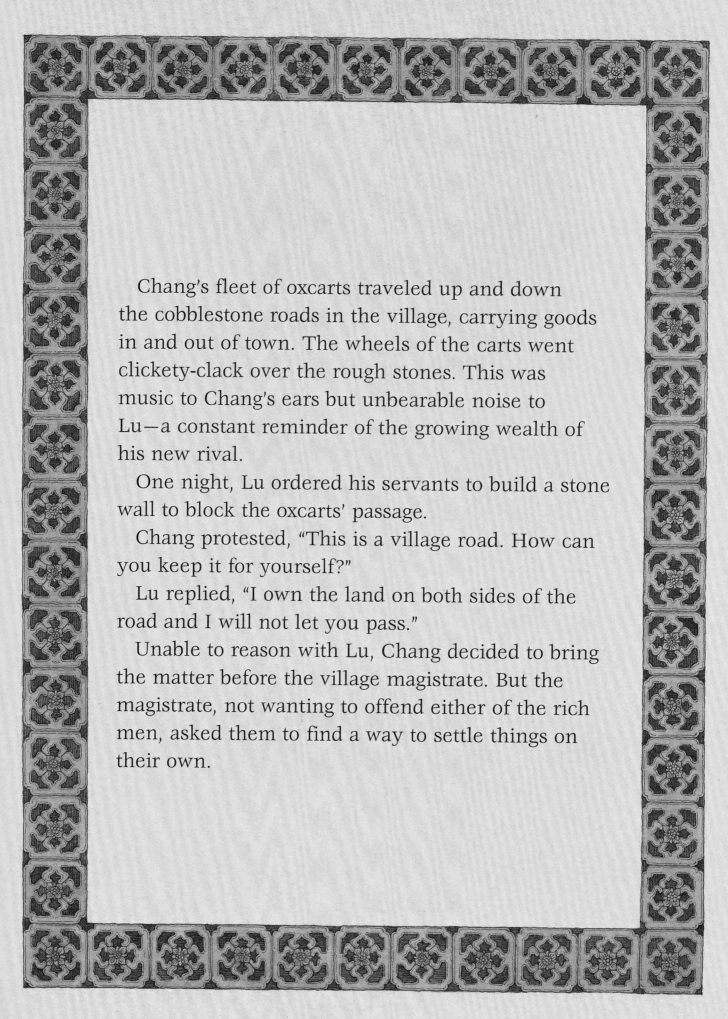

Chang's fleet of oxcarts traveled up and down the cobblestone roads in the village, carrying goods in and out of town. The wheels of the carts went clickety-clack over the rough stones. This was music to Chang's ears but unbearable noise to Lu—a constant reminder of the growing wealth of his new rival.

One night, Lu ordered his servants to build a stone wall to block the oxcarts' passage.

Chang protested, "This is a village road. How can you keep it for yourself?"

Lu replied, "I own the land on both sides of the road and I will not let you pass."

Unable to reason with Lu, Chang decided to bring the matter before the village magistrate. But the magistrate, not wanting to offend either of the rich men, asked them to find a way to settle things on their own.

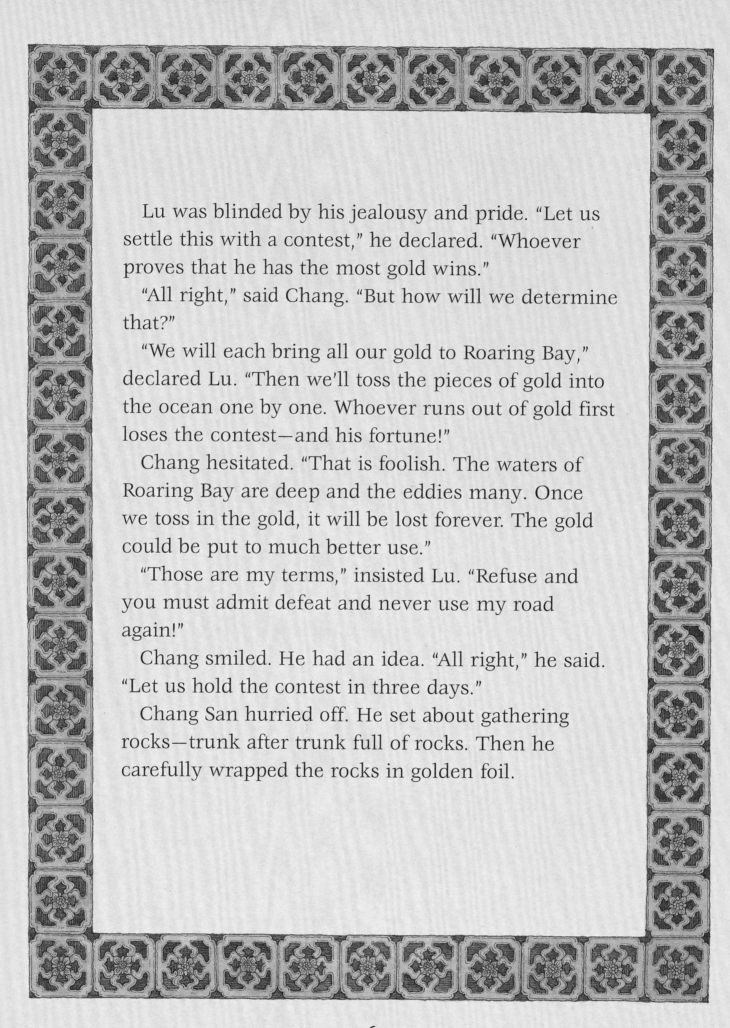

Lu was blinded by his jealousy and pride. "Let us settle this with a contest," he declared. "Whoever proves that he has the most gold wins."

"All right," said Chang. "But how will we determine that?"

"We will each bring all our gold to Roaring Bay," declared Lu. "Then we'll toss the pieces of gold into the ocean one by one. Whoever runs out of gold first loses the contest—and his fortune!"

Chang hesitated. "That is foolish. The waters of Roaring Bay are deep and the eddies many. Once we toss in the gold, it will be lost forever. The gold could be put to much better use."

"Those are my terms," insisted Lu. "Refuse and you must admit defeat and never use my road again!"

Chang smiled. He had an idea. "All right," he said. "Let us hold the contest in three days."

Chang San hurried off. He set about gathering rocks—trunk after trunk full of rocks. Then he carefully wrapped the rocks in golden foil.

Another year passed. On the second day of the Chinese New Year, Lee, Yomei, and D.K. visited Master Liu, taking along some pieces of gold as a gift. Since they didn't want to appear showy, they packed the gold at the bottom of Lee's baskets, then piled snails on top.

When they arrived, Yomei's sisters and their husbands were already there. They had brought Master Liu elegant, expensive gifts and began to ridicule Yomei and Lee for their humble and very smelly offering.

Master Liu was also annoyed. Yomei's sisters were dressed in their finest gowns, but Yomei wore a plain old dress. "No wonder her sisters pick on her," he grumbled.

After a sumptuous New Year's banquet, the family sat around the table and chatted. Damei and Amei's husbands bragged about their wealth, trying to top one another

"I'm tired of being a landlord. It's such a burden to own so much land," said one.

"Yes indeed!" replied the other. "It's quite exhausting. I wish I could sell it all, put my feet up, and relax."

Lee spoke up. "You don't want your land anymore? I would gladly buy it."

The two men thought this was very funny and decided to play along with the foolish peddler. They drew up a contract and asked Master Liu to be the witness. They even offered to sell for half-price and sat back waiting for Lee to make a fool of himself.

To their astonishment, Lee removed the snails from the top of his baskets and poured the gold onto the table. The two brothers-in-law could not believe their eyes! "How can this be?" they cried. "Where did Lee get so much money?" They wrung their hands and moaned, filled with regret for having sold their land so cheaply.

Lee explained about the black gold and handed the contract to Master Liu. "The gold was supposed to be our gift to you," he said. "Please accept the land instead."

Cuddling his beloved grandson on his lap, Master Liu sat silently, deep in thought. Finally he set D.K. in one of the baskets and turned to Yomei. "You and your husband humble me with your generosity. But I cannot accept this gift. Let us donate the land to the people of the village."

Yomei smiled up at her father. "Are you sure?" she asked.

"Yes," Liu replied. "You have already given me the greatest treasure of all—your love and devotion."

From that day on, Master Liu was a changed man. He was no longer snobbish. He helped the poor and took delight in simple pleasures. And he lived happily ever after, along with Yomei, Lee, and his precious grandson.

金玉滿堂

大吉

吉祥

大利

如意

五福臨門

Notes on the Stories

The story "Auntie Tigress" has been popular throughout China for hundreds of years. It may have originated as a tale told by the Hakka people. "The Fisherman and the Tycoon" and "The Greatest Treasure" are stories that originated in the coastal provinces of China, most likely Fujian Province.

While the stories in this book have the universal appeal of all good folktales, they do contain some details that may not be familiar to Western readers.

PAGE 4

In Chinese folklore, there exists a traditional theme of animals and plants that, having lived on Earth for thousands of years, have absorbed the essence of Heaven, Earth, Sun, and Moon and thus develop the ability to transform themselves into human forms. The bad spirits of such animals and plants, like Auntie Tigress, would exploit their morphing powers to prey on humans. The good spirits would long to become part of human society, and would try hard to blend in.

PAGE 6

The Chinese characters on the piece of red paper on the door of MeiMei's house, *Fu*, stand for good fortune. To welcome in the Lunar New Year, the Chinese often paste characters or stanzas calling for good fortune, health, and other wishes on their front doors. These festive decorations would generally stay on until the next New Year.

PAGE 9

The buns shown here are steamed treats made of leavened dough. They may be made without filling or wrapped around meat or sweet ingredients such as red bean paste. Buns and dumplings, as they are frequently referred to in English, are almost interchangeable, but Chinese dumplings often refer to ravioli-like treats made of dough and filled with meat, shrimp, vegetables, or combinations of all three ingredients.

PAGE 21

The distinctive boatlike shape of the gold shown in the chest was the form used for currency in China for centuries. Gold, silver, and tin were cast in this shape in different sizes, each size and metal having a different monetary value.

PAGE 32

Incorporated into the art in the border is the *Shuang Xi* character, which is a combination of two happiness characters commonly used at weddings, birthday banquets, and other joyful occasions.

PAGE 33

In parts of China, snails are considered a delicacy, just like *escargot* in French cuisine. They can be found in fields and along the edges of rice paddies.

PAGE 36

The two posters above the door knockers are portraits of the Guardians of Doors. According to legend, malicious spirits disturbed the sleep of an emperor from the Tang dynasty. His two most trusted generals decided to stand guard outside the palace doors to prevent the spirits from intruding on the emperor's peace. Since then, people have hung paintings of the two generals on their doors to protect their families from evil.

The frame around the text and illustration includes a picture of gourds tied with blue ribbons. Gourds traditionally symbolize good fortune and health. (The Chinese word for *gourd* is a close homonym to *Fu*, the same good-luck character that was pasted on MeiMei's front door.) Gourds were also used by many herbalists to carry and store their medicines, so the gourd image often represents people's wish for a long and healthy life.

PAGE 39

The patch on the boy's head is a homemade bandage. This is traditionally a small piece of cloth with herbal ointment in the center that is used for superficial wounds.

PAGE 40

The two red banners on the sides of the front doors are known as *Chun Lian*, which roughly translates to *springtime stanzas*. These short verses convey wishes for good fortune, good health, etc. Chinese hang these banners just before the Lunar New Year. The stanzas in the illustration are two of the most popular, expressing the hope for "living long lives as the years go by" and "a home filled with joy as spring arrives."

PAGE 42

Incorporated into the art in the border are four traditional Chinese phrases that reflect the celebratory mood and happy ending of the story.